Funny Things I Heard at the Bus Stop: Volume 1

ANGELA GIROUX

DEDICATION

This book is dedicated to Max and Sophie, the inspiration for all of the wonderful stories that I want to share with everyone.

Contents

Prologue

8:30 am. Monday morning. Time to leave for school.

"Don't forget your lunch pack!" yells Mom. Dad already packed my sandwich earlier that morning (a TBRL – turkey, bacon, ranch, and lettuce) but today they had a nacho haystack on the menu and Linda the Lunch Lady always gave me an extra scoop of that ooey-gooey creamy deliciousness known as nacho cheese (although I use the term "cheese" loosely). It's my stomach's best friend, next to maybe a filet mignon, medium rare. My taste buds just can't get enough of that orange stuff!

I reluctantly grab my lunch pack and head out the door. "C'mon, Sophie! We're gonna be late!" I scream as my sister finishes brushing her hair and making sure that she has her pink zebra-print duct tape in her backpack. She and her friend Nicole love making things out of duct tape – wallets, purses, hair bows, picture frames – you name it. And don't tell her, but I think the stuff she makes is super cool.

We head on out and start the trek to the bus stop. A good six blocks or so to get there. For a first grader it's probably a long walk, but not for me. Especially since by the time we get to the bus stop there's no less than eight of us, sometimes ten or more. We live in a cul-de-sac and the long walk goes past four or five other kids' houses that ride the bus. So Sophie and I are kinda like the train engine (I'm of course the engineer and Sophie is just the one that rings the bell) and along the way more freight cars keep getting added. It all starts with us. So we HAVE to leave on time.

Just three houses down we pick up David. He's in my class in fifth grade. He's a gamer like me, but plays more games on the computer than he does video games. He's like a coal car because of his dark black hair. Then next we pick up Sophie's friend Emma and her brother Joey. Emma is a very interesting girl. She thinks she's in high school like her sisters. And Joey is a fun kid. He puked once on my dad's back at the circus. I guess Emma would be a boxcar and Joey would be the hobo hiding in it.

On down the next block we go past Eric's house. Eric will probably end up being a mayor or maybe the president of a company or even the country. He's very diplomatic. He would probably be a passenger car on our bus stop train. Another block and across the street and we're at Nicole's house. Nicole is really cool and super nice. I guess she would be the oil tanker, for no other reason than we need to have one and she might as well be the one. Finally we come to Riley's house. Riley gets to be the caboose, but only because he's the last one to join our group on the walk to the bus stop.

Another couple blocks and we make it to the bus stop.

The bus comes at 8:50 so we have a good twenty minutes to kill as we make the journey from our house to the yellow submarine of knowledge as I like to call it. Along the way we do lots of things to make the walk more fun. We have snowball fights in the winter. We throw acorns at the squirrels. We sing songs. We race to the stop sign. And we tell stories. Lots of stories.

I've heard so many stories on that walk to the bus stop, and so many more just waiting for the bus when we get there early that I bet I could write a book about it and pass along all the stories to you. So that's what I'm doing.

The six stories here are some of my very best favorites. They are more for kids my age but I'm sure the younger kids will enjoy them, too. Anyway, bus is coming......enjoy!

The Last Napkin

The scene: a napkin factory. The machines spin, fold, stamp, and pack huge rolls of paper products into the final product and ultimate goal of everyone in the plant - a napkin.

What starts out as a giant roll of "one big happy family" fibrous material has now been manhandled and twisted into individual one or two-ply squares of mouth-wiping cloth. Each napkin says goodbye to his community of raw paper and now gets packed like a sardine in plastic with 199 other napkins for their journey to the distribution outlet, grocery store, and eventually your home.

But think about the last little napkin at the bottom of the pack. Poor little guy is squished tightly at the very end of the napkin train with his butt exposed to the world. Sure, the guy at the top is exposed, too, but at least he can see where he's going.

You might think that the ones in the middle have it worse since they just stare at the napkin in front of them and are getting squished from behind by the rest of the pack. But when they are packed into a larger box with other packs of napkins, the last napkin is now on the bottom, feeling the weight of the other 199 napkins. Right in his face.

Eventually they make it to the grocery store, super mart, pharmacy, or other store that will put the napkin pack on the shelf with other packs. Again, the last napkin's butt is proudly displayed for all to see. How embarrassing. Without having to strain too much, the last napkin is still able to see a little to his right or left. Too much trying to stare in one direction without moving his head gets to be a real pain in the brain though.

Yay! Today is the day! A nice young woman of mid-thirtiesh grabs the last napkin's pack. Too bad for the middle guys. They are getting squeezed and smushed while the last napkin sits back and laughs. Whoops, spoke too soon. A two liter bottle of Coke just landed on the pack. "Hey, quit pushing!" They're all going to have headaches after this.

Finally the pack makes it back to the house. It is days before any napkin gets a breath of fresh air. Finally someone rips open the pack and grabs a handful of napkins. Later fellas! The top napkin and his posse are off to the napkin holder. Tonight is spaghetti so all of their training will pay off for sure. Especially since this house has three kids under seven years old.

A week later and the last napkin is still in the pack. He and his buddies talk about what kinds of food they think they are going to be experiencing. Pizza? Meatloaf? Maybe a nice shrimp scampi with a real drippy garlic butter sauce? Oh, if only wishes could come true. Or maybe they will get to be a not-so-quicker-picker-upper when someone spills a glass of milk. And the chances of that are pretty high with preschoolers around.

The day is almost here. The last napkin has spent weeks preparing for his one big performance. The last group has been tasked for duty and put in the napkin container. Crap. He's on the bottom again. Well, not so bad this time. He's used to it. One by one his buddies get called into duty: mac and cheese, cupcakes, lasagna (that one had a lot of his friends working hard), some spilled grape juice, tartar sauce.

There are now only a handful - let's see, one, two, three, four - napkins ahead of him ready to wipe up, clean, or get tossed into the trash like a three point shot from the line. Dinner time. The last napkin is ready. It's gonna be a good day, too. Chili and grilled cheese. Bound to be plenty of beans, sauce, or chunks of ground beef splattered all over the table, floor, shirts, and mouths.

Oops...someone knocked over their milk. Go figure. Yes! A big glop of chili just fell on Bobby's shirt. Woo hoo! That glop made it to the table and even some on the floor. Looks like a multiple-napkin job for sure. Now there's only one napkin left. The last napkin.

Wait. Where's she going? The lady that manhandled the napkin squadron just a week or so ago just went in the basement. Oh no. Another pack of napkins. What is she doing? Is she opening up that pack? But there's still one left! Wait...don't forget about...

Crap.

The last napkin is now 51st in line. A brand new bunch of

recruits smashes the last napkin. If he could cry he would. All that training. All of the preparation. For what? A week later, the same story. When will it end?

The last napkin has finally accepted his mission. He's the last napkin. That's his job. And he does it well.

A Visit From Nonna Esmeralda

Aidan woke up bright and early, even before his twin brother, Hayden, still snoring away in the top level of their shared bunk bed. Aidan's first thought of the day was that his grandmother was arriving for a visit! She lived far, far away, in a warm and sunny country called Italy, and this was the very first time ever that he would meet her. From all the stories he had heard about her travels around the world, she sounded pretty amazing. Aidan dreamed of becoming a world-traveler himself...maybe even an OUT-of this-world traveler, like an astronaut! He couldn't wait to hear his grandmother, whose name was Nonna Esmeralda, tell her travel tales.

Grabbing his favorite Batman robe and tip-toeing out the door, Aidan took off, full speed, down the stairs toward the kitchen where his mother was making breakfast. "Nonna Esmeralda's coming today!" he cried, bounding into the room and tripping over Gypsy, the little rat terrier, stretched out across the doorway. Aidan's dad, seated at the breakfast table, caught him just in time. "Hold on there, buddy--you don't want to meet your grandmother for the very first time with a big goose egg on your head!"

Aidan settled down at his place at the table, pushing

away the orange juice that was waiting for him there. "When will she be here, Mom?" he asked. "Do you think she'll like me? And can I have Coolio-Aid instead of this stupid juice?" His mother sighed, and then smiled. "Drink your juice, please. And of course Nonna will like you, honey. She's as excited to meet you as you are to meet her! Your Auntie Maria already picked her up at the airport--they're on their way here right now."

Aidan was SO excited to meet his grandmother that he just couldn't sit still, and wiggled around in his chair, almost knocking over his juice. Nonna Esmeralda was his mother's mom, and he had grown up hearing lots of fascinating stories about her. His dad said that she was a "gypsy" and had travelled all over the world. Aidan had named his little dog "Gypsy" because of it. He also hoped to travel all over the world with Gypsy, having wild adventures just like his Nonna Esmeralda did with her big, black cat, Magus.

Aidan's mom brought over a steaming bowl of oatmeal, with cream and melted butter making a little lake on the top. There were wrinkly raisins poking up from the "lake" as well, and it reminded Aidan of the pictures he'd seen in his 3rd grade history book of brown wooly mammoths stuck in the La Brea Tar Pits. He began to carefully save the wooly mammoths with his spoon, and then sneaked them under the table for Gypsy. When the mammoths were all gone, Aidan began sending spoonfuls of the Tar Pits under the table to his greedy little dog. They made great partners; Gypsy would eat absolutely anything; she'd once even downed a full box of rubber bands!

Aidan didn't like ANYTHING for breakfast except the very best cereal in the entire world, Yucky Charms. He must've told his parents this about a zillion times, but his mom's idea of "good for you" stuff just kept showing up on his plate. He'd stopped trying to convince his parents that Yucky Charms were good for him...it made him HAPPY, and happiness is good for you! But if he could get Gypsy to keep on being his under-the-table chowhound, Aidan was ok with that. He kept a secret stash of Yucky Charms in his closet, bought with money he'd recently gotten for his 9th birthday. As long as he could sneak a couple of sticky, gooey, heavenly handfuls after "eating" his stupid Healthy Breakfast, he was good to go!

Gypsy started making loud slurping noises under the table, and his mother gave Aidan a funny look. He began busily stirring his oatmeal, making sure to clank his spoon loudly against the sides of the bowl, and then burst out into song .... although he really wasn't at all sure what he was singing. He just needed to do something...anything....FAST in order to distract his parents before they discovered the REAL reason that Gypsy had grown so fat in the past few months!

Waving his spoon around like a crazed conductor, and belting it out at the top of his lungs, Aidan sang:

"Dear Nonna Esmeralda,
I am so glad to greetcha.

There's lots I wanna tell ya,
But first, I gotta meetcha!
 I hear you come from Naples,
And live upon a farm.
My favorite trees are maples...
And I love Yucky Charms!"

By the time that Aidan got to the last line of his silly song, he had gotten very worked up. SO worked up, in fact, that the "big finish" of smashing his spoon on the table was the finish of his cereal bowl as well. The spoon hit its edge, and still filled with oatmeal, the bowl went flying across the kitchen and smashed hard against the wall. Aidan watched, horrified as it exploded into dozens of fragments, flinging bits of sticky oatmeal everywhere. Absolutely everywhere; including right on the nose of Nonna Esmeralda, who had just stepped into the kitchen, with Auntie Maria standing wide-eyed and open-mouthed behind her!

Everyone froze. Nobody made a sound, including Gypsy, who was cowering under the table. And then, to Aidan's amazement, Nonna Esmeralda smiled and began singing the exact same song he'd been singing before she even got there, but with different words:

"My Dearest Grandson, Aidan,
I'm also glad to greetcha.
Your brother's name is Hayden,

And I came here to meetcha.
 It's true, I come from Naples,
And live upon a farm.
Back home, we don't have maples,
But we have Yucky Charms!"

How in the world did she know his song, when not even HE knew it?

Nonna Esmeralda gave Aidan a very tight hug, which surprised him. Not only because he had just covered her with sticky bits of flying oatmeal, but because she was so tiny, not even as tall as himself. But was she ever strong! He sat back down at the table while the other grown-ups fussed over her, taking her big pink and orange polka-dotted suitcase, her funny purple hat with the big green flowers, and her bright blue coat and long, sunflower-yellow scarf. This left her fairly oatmeal-free, except for the one big blob still stuck to her long nose.

Nonna saw that Aidan was staring at her, and she crossed her eyes and looked down her nose to see what the matter was. "Aha!" she cried, picking off the last piece of sodden cereal. "Your breakfast! Do you want this back, Bambino mio?" Aidan shook his head violently. "Oh, no, Nonna, I don't like oatmeal....or anything..." Nonna Esmeralda finished his sentence for him; "...except for Yucky Charms, is that right?" "Exactly!" replied Aidan. "My parents don't think they're good for me. But they ARE good....they make me happy!"

Nonna Esmeralda thought about this for a moment and then sat down at the table while the other adults bustled about, cleaning the oatmeal from her clothing....and the floor....the wall.....the ceiling....and even Stubbs, the half-tailed cat who'd been napping on the counter when the bowl hit. Nonna took Aidan's hand in her own and turned it over, palm side up, furrowing her forehead as she studied the lines on it. "Yes, Bambino. Happiness is a good thing. But sometimes we must learn for ourselves what real happiness is. And sometimes we must learn the hard way."

Aidan didn't know what she was talking about...and he also didn't know why she was calling him "Bambino." "Nonna, what does "Bambino" mean?" She smiled and replied, "Ah, that is just my way of telling you how much you mean to me. It means "child" in Italian, and you are my very special child, caro mio. Oh! There is some more Italian for you. "Caro mio" means "my dear". And you and your family are VERY dear to me!"

Just then, Aidan's brother Hayden came into the kitchen, rubbing his eyes...and then rubbing them again when he saw Nonna Esmeralda, and also all the oatmeal still stuck to the ceiling. Nonna Esmeralda got up and gave her other grandson a hug as tight as the one she'd given Aidan. Hayden's eyes bulged a bit, but he looked happy to finally meet his colorful grandmother. "Why did it take so long for us to meet you, Nonna?" he asked. "Oh, that is a story for another time, caro mio," she replied. "Why don't we all go into the living room, so

I can show you what I've brought?" "Presents???" both Aidan and Hayden cried out at the same time. They tried to get through the kitchen doorway at the same time, with Gypsy tangled under their feet, barking wildly at all the excitement.

As soon as everyone was settled in the living room, Nonna Esmeralda opened up her suitcase. Inside and out, it was all the colors of the rainbow; a bright pink silk scarf embroidered with orange butterflies, a vivid yellow-and purple-striped long silk skirt, a pair of orange leather boots, and a blue cape with little green elephants dancing all over it! There were also some very intriguing bags and boxes wrapped in shiny cloth instead of paper. "I always wrap gifts in fabric," said Nonna Esmeralda, as she began lifting things out of the overflowing suitcase. "That way, it's like getting TWO gifts instead of just one!" Aidan and Hayden watched in amazement as Nonna kept on taking gift after gift out of the case. "How did she manage to get so much stuff into that thing?" Aidan thought to himself. Maybe what he once overheard his father say to his mother about Nonna knowing magic was actually true!

His thoughts were interrupted by Nonna's voice, speaking to his brother; "Here, Bambino; this is for you. I got it when I was in Egypt." "Wow," thought Aidan, "Egypt! Nonna really HAS gotten around!" Hayden untied the silky green material and opened the box. "Cool!!!" he shouted, holding up a gleaming golden pyramid. "I LOVE Egyptian stuff!" That was totally true, Aidan thought. Hayden was a

15

complete freak about pharaohs and mummies and pyramids and everything else about ancient Egyptian. He wanted to be an archeologist someday and discover buried temples and the treasures they still held. Nonna Esmeralda showed Hayden a secret compartment in the pyramid which contained a tiny mummy in a brightly painted tomb, and little figures of the ancient gods and goddess of Egypt. Hayden was beyond thrilled. "SUPERcoolio!" he shouted. "Thanks SO much, Nonna!"

His grandmother looked pleased, then resumed passing out more gifts; a beautiful gold silk robe from Japan for his mother, a pair of heavy silver bookends from Peru for his father, and a magnificent necklace of deep purple amethysts from Russia for his Auntie Maria. "Nonna Esmeralda really must be a gypsy to have travelled so much," Aidan thought. Oh, the adventures she must have had! How he would love to take such incredible journeys himself. His parents always told him to be patient; that after he graduated school he could experience all the places he now only dreamed about through books and the internet. But when you're nine, "after graduation" is an ETERNITY to wait...maybe even LONGER!

Nonna Esmeralda continued to pass out wonderful presents from her bottomless suitcase. Then, finally, at looooong last, it was Aidan's turn. Maybe she'd saved the best for the last? He was just about to come out of his skin with the excitement of seeing his own incredible gift. Everyone else's had been absolutely perfect! And now Nonna Esmeralda reached one last time into her suitcase, deep, deep down, and pulled out a box, wrapped in fabric that shone like the sun and the moon combined; both gold and silver at the same time. "For you, caro Bambino," she said, placing it into his lap. "I think that you will really like it." Aidan couldn't wait to see what lay inside. If it was anything like what the rest of his family had received, it was going to be CRAZY cool! "Thanks, Nonna!" he said, struggling to untie the knotted fabric, which finally gave way, revealing a surprisingly plain wooden box.

He kept thinking about what his mom always told him - "Don't judge a book by its cover." Maybe what lay inside was even MORE spectacular than any of the other's gifts! "I know I'm REALLY going to love it! How do you know the absolutely perfect things to give to....?" Aidan's voice suddenly dropped away as he opened the lid. There, wrapped in what looked to be old, dried leaves, was a small brown clay bowl. With a chip on the edge and a small crack running along one side. Aidan lifted it up and looked back into the box. There HAD to be something else in there! But no, all that the box contained was this stupid, ugly bowl. He couldn't remember ever feeling so disappointed, almost to the point of tears. Everyone else had gotten such GREAT presents! Why would Nonna Esmeralda give him such an awful gift? Maybe she didn't like him so much after all. Maybe "Bambino" REALLY meant "rat-faced dork boy"!

Nonna Esmeralda could see the look of disbelief on his face, and she gently took the bowl from his hands. "Caro mio....do not judge things always by their appearance. There may be much beauty in what at first appears to be ugly. And small things can be very powerful. And also practical; from what I saw when I first walked into the kitchen today, I think you could use a new cereal bowl!" Aidan was still speechless, fighting back his tears. How could this little cracked bowl even hold more than just a few spoonfuls of cereal...and the milk would probably leak out of it, too!

Suddenly, hot tears exploded from his eyes and ran down his face. "Aidan!" scolded his father. "That is no way to receive a gift!" His mother and aunt look equally disapproving and even Hayden was shaking his head. But Nonna Esmeralda gently took Aidan's hand. "No, no...it is just fine. This is not a very impressive gift, I know. Well....not yet, anyway." She stood up and raised Aidan to his feet, then walked towards the kitchen. "We are going to go and see if his new cereal bowl actually works. We will see you all in a little while."

Aidan slowly followed Nonna Esmeralda into the kitchen, with Gypsy following along behind. He sat at the table while Nonna scurried about, putting this and that into a pot on the stove, while he glared at the stupid little clay thing, sitting lopsidedly in front of him. He still didn't understand how he could have gotten such a ridiculous gift, especially when everyone else's had been so fantastic. Why didn't Nonna Esmeralda like him? He'd never done anything bad to her. It just wasn't fair!

And now, it was going to get worse, because she was

coming to the table with a big, steaming bowl of what looked like purple oatmeal with chunks of something bright green in it! Aidan thought he might start crying again....or, even worse, throw up! Even Gypsy wasn't begging for any of THAT horrible stuff! "Give me your bowl, Bambino mio," said Nonna. "But do not eat anything until we have had a chance to talk." "HAH!" thought Aidan. "Not a problem—there's NO WAY I'm going to be putting ANY of that garbage in my mouth!" But he didn't say anything as his grandmother ladled spoonful after spoonful of the strange, slimy stuff into the little bowl. How was it managing to contain so much? Apparently, it was like her weird suitcase ...a bottomless pit!

The little bowl was finally full...and the pot empty, which made NO sense whatsoever. But not much about this day was making sense any more, at least not to Aidan. "You're a little disappointed in your gift, aren't you, caro mio?" Nonna Esmeralda gently asked, handing him her polka-dotted handkerchief. Aidan blotted his eyes and nodded miserably. He knew it wasn't polite to be ungrateful for a gift, even THIS one, but somehow, he just couldn't pretend with his grandmother. She smiled and patted his hand." I understand. When my own grandmother, your GranNonna Isabella, first gave this little bowl to me, I was also unhappy about it. But I learned quickly that appearances can be VERY deceiving!" Aidan started to feel less disappointed and more interested. This bowl had been passed down through generations? Hmm...maybe it wasn't entirely lame after all.

Nonna continued; "You know I have travelled all over the world, yes, Bambino? But I don't think you know HOW I have done it, do you?" Aidan said he guessed that she did it like everyone else; plane, train, car, boat...maybe a donkey or camel every now and then? Nonna Esmeralda laughed and then whispered, "No, caro mio.....I did it all with this little bowl!" Aidan's eyes grew wide, and he straightened up to stare at his apparently loony grandmother. How in the world could she have travelled in this strange little bowl? That was just nuts! But he had to admit, this was no ordinary bowl. If it could fit a whole big pot of purple oatmeal inside, could it also fit Nonna Esmeralda? He didn't know WHAT to think anymore!

Nonna Esmeralda had stopped laughing. She was looking very seriously at him, and Aidan suddenly felt that she could actually read his mind with her dark, unblinking eyes. There were strange, beautiful gold flecks swimming in their chocolate depths, and he found it impossible to look away. His grandmother spoke in a low voice; "What I am about to tell you, Bambino, you cannot tell to anyone. Not even your mama or papa....and especially not your brother." Aidan often kept secrets from his big-mouthed brother, but his parents, too? "Yes, even your parents," said Nonna, seeming to again read his mind. "You will understand once I explain to you what this little bowl can do. So, caro mio....do you promise?" Aidan found himself nodding and gulping hard at the same time. He didn't feel good about keeping secrets from his parents, but he trusted Nonna Esmeralda. And he was just so, SO eager to learn the secret of his bowl!

"Good!" said his grandmother, the gold in her eyes twinkling brightly. Now, listen to me very carefully. Because it is possible that your life could depend upon it!" "Hey, wait just a minute!" thought Aidan. This was starting to sound more dangerous than exciting. But, before he had a chance to say anything out loud, Nonna continued. "This bowl, caro mio, has been in our family for longer than anyone can remember. Long before your country became the United States....even before Christopher Columbus came here." Aidan interrupted; "Christopher Columbus came to Chicago?" His teacher, Miss Percival, had never taught his class at Polk Elementary THAT interesting piece of information! "No, no, caro mio," Nonna laughed, "He never came here to Chicago...it didn't even exist back then!

No one knows how old this bowl is. Perhaps as old as the ancient days of the Roman Empire. Perhaps even older!" "Wow!" Aidan thought "Maybe my bowl is even older than the pyramids and mummies! Wouldn't THAT make Hayden jealous!" His grandmother interrupted his thoughts. "Aidan, pay attention to what I am telling you and don't be thinking about making your brother jealous." Aidan's eyes grew to their very widest. Nonna Esmeralda's lips hadn't moved even the tiniest bit! How in the world had he heard her? And how had SHE heard HIM?

Nonna Esmeralda continued; "Bambino, you must treat

this bowl, which is called the Teleportraveling Bowl, with the very greatest respect. It can take you, as it has me, on the most marvelous adventures, whenever and wherever you desire. But ONLY if you treat it properly! If you do not, there is no telling what may happen. Do you understand?" Aidan tried to reply, but found that his voice had disappeared completely. He wanted to go on these marvelous adventures more than ANYTHING else in the entire world! He nodded his head up and down like a bobble-head doll on a trampoline. "Yes! Yes!" The words suddenly burst out of him; "I'll do exactly as you say--tell me! Tell me!"

His grandmother put a cautioning finger to her lips and looked toward the kitchen door. From the living room came the sound of his family's favorite TV show; "Wild World Wanderings With Wilbur Wombat." He and Nonna could both yell at the top of their voices and nobody would notice while THAT program was on. The entire family loved to dream of world travels, and now Nonna Esmeralda was telling him that he was going to have the most amazing travels of them all!

"How long does that television show last, Bambino?" his grandmother asked. "Half an hour," he replied. "Perfecto! That is exactly the right time for your first adventure," she said. "But, Nonna," he protested, "Even on my bike, I couldn't get more than 10 blocks away and back in only half an hour! What kind of adventure is THAT?" Nonna's eyes twinkled like golden stars, "Ah, but remember, caro; you are not going to be travelling on your bike. You will be travelling in this!" She held up the little clay bowl, and Aidan could swear that some of the gold from her eyes leaped down into it.

She placed it carefully into his hands, and he looked inside. Yep—there WERE little speckles of fiery gold dancing on top of the purple oatmeal! And the green stuff was beginning to glow even greener! In fact, the entire bowl was beginning to get very warm in his hands, and even vibrate a little. "What's happening, Nonna?" he cried with alarm. "Listen to me, Aidan," Nonna replied. "There isn't much time before you take off on your first adventure. When I tell you, concentrate very hard on the place you wish to be, and picture yourself actually there." "Can it be anywhere?" Aidan asked? "Anywhere and anytime as well." replied his grandmother. "But for now, chose someplace nearby and right now....just in case." "Ok," Aidan agreed. He'd been planning on focusing on ancient Egypt and bringing Hayden back a REAL mummy, but maybe Nonna was right. That was asking a whole lot for his first time out—and what if he got stuck?! Better save the "big stuff" for later.

Instead, he decided to just picture himself at the local shopping center, the River Front Mall. Even if he couldn't get back home by using the bowl, it was still within walking distance. He told his grandmother what he'd chosen, and she nodded approvingly. "A good choice, Bambino. Now, when I tell you, you are going to picture yourself there, in a safe place, and then take a bite of the special cereal in your bowl." Aidan squinted his eyes at the lumpy purple, green-chunked stuff and made a face. If it looked this awful, what was it going to taste like? "Oh, by the way," his grandmother continued, "you can decide what you want it to taste like, and it will be just that very thing!" "Whew!" thought Aidan. "Thank goodness for that!" He asked out loud, "Nonna, how will I get back home again?" "Easy, caro... just the same way as you got there. So, you must never forget the secret words; and also make sure you don't leave the bowl behind or it will be your very last trip ever! Are you ready?"

Aidan reached for a pen from off the table and got ready to write on his arm. "Ready, Nonna!" he said. Nonna Esmeralda drew closer and whispered in his ear. The magic words flowed from her lips and into his ear, tickling with little breathy fingers, then making their way into his mind, where they bounced around like playful puppies; "Eamus turpis!" he heard. "What did that mean?" Aidan wondered. He scribbled it down as best he could on his arm, and then showed it to his grandmother. "Very close, Bambino! Just one little change..." She took the pen and changed what he'd written from "turnips" to "turpis." "There! Perfecto! Now, we haven't much time. The TV show will be over in 20 minutes, and you must be back before it ends. Are you ready for your first adventure?" Aidan nodded, a bit nervously, but the excitement of it all outweighed his fear. "Ready, Nonna!" he said, spooning up a big blob of the purple oatmeal and willing it to taste like his beloved Yucky Charms.

At the same time, he pictured himself standing by the big

fountain in the center of the River Front Mall, next to the food court. "Now, Aidan..say the words!", said his grandmother. "Eamus turpis!" he cried out, before shoving the purple blob into his mouth. He swallowed, amazed. It DID taste JUST like his beloved Yucky Charms, just like Nonna Esmeralda had said it would! Suddenly, his head began to feel woozy, and the room began to spin. He closed his eyes and held on tight to the little bowl, which suddenly began to grow, bigger and bigger. Or...was HE shrinking smaller and smaller? Aidan couldn't tell...all he knew was that SOMETHING really strange was happening!

There was a bump...and then a thump...and Aidan was suddenly aware of the sound of a lot of people talking. And of water splashing! His eyes flew open--and there, directly in front of him, was the big fountain in the center of the River Front Mall, the water shining brightly with all the colored lights just below the pool's surface. He stood there for a few minutes, still a bit woozy from the experience, slowly taking it all in. The little bowl rested in his trembling hands, still full of its sloppy purple contents. Shoppers walked past him like nothing was at all unusual...like he had arrived there just as they had.

Aidan stared down at the little bowl. It had actually worked! He could travel wherever he wanted, and Nonna Esmeralda had said it could even be through time! His head began to spin even faster at the thought...where would he go to next time? A castle in the Middle Ages? The signing of the

Declaration of Independence? On the Titanic before it hit the iceberg? Could he warn the captain in time?

"Hey, Aidan!" He turned his head at the sound of his name, which made him even dizzier. He quickly shoved the Teleportraveling Bowl deep into his coat pocket, taking care to keep it upright. Oh, nooooo! Of ALL the people to run into! Puzzy MacFadden, the school know-it-all, was standing behind him, eating a big, drippy Blueberry Blast double-dip ice cream cone, half of it running down the front of his neon orange and black-striped t-shirt. He filled it out almost to bursting, which made him look like an ice-cream-cone-eating Halloween pumpkin. "Whatcha doin', Aidan?" Puzzy asked. "Ya wanna hang out?" Nonna Esmeralda's voice spoke clearly in his head; "You must be back before the television show ends!" How much time had passed already? He had no idea...but Puzzy had a big cartoon character watch strapped tightly around his thick wrist. "Um...maybe," Aidan replied. "Hey, what time is it, anyway?" Puzzy consulted his watch. "It's only 10:15. My mom isn't picking me up until 1:30. We have LOTS of time to hang out here!" That gave Aidan fifteen minutes before he had to get back into the Teleportraveling Bowl. But now he had nosey Puzzy to deal with. How was he going to ditch the biggest blabbermouth in all of Polk Elementary School before time ran out?

Now Puzzy was pulling his wallet out of the pocket of his orange plaid sweatpants, opening it to show Aidan the crisp $10 bill inside. "It was my birthday last week," he said. "My grandma gave me this and said I could do whatever I wanted with it. Wanna go get some Choco-Cheezies? I'll treat you! I'll even buy you TWO!" Ohhhhhh, mannnnn! If there was any junk food that Aidan loved, it was Choco-Cheezies! It sounded disgusting, he knew, but somehow, the thick cheddar cheese and sweet milk chocolate managed to blend together amazingly! He sure wished he could tell Puzzy what HIS gift from his grandmother had been, but that would be the same as telling the entire world!

Aidan found himself nodding "yes" and following Puzzy toward the delightful smells of the food court. Choco-Cheezies had a magic power all of their own! But once in line, he began to worry. What if they didn't get their orders in time and he materialized back in the kitchen surrounded by his shocked family? Would Nonna Esmeralda take away the bowl? He asked Puzzy once again for the time. "Geez, Aidan...what's your rush? It's Saturday morning and we have the whole weekend ahead of us!" But finally, he told him the time; 10:20. Uh, oh....that only left ten minutes to get back...and there were still 5 people in line ahead of them!

Aidan didn't know what to do. If he left now and found a quiet place to "go bowling"; as he'd decided to call his magical travelling, then he could get back home in plenty of time, no problem! But that meant no Choco-Cheezies; and they sure didn't come his way very often. His parents called them "beyond nasty" and refused to buy them. He would have to save up a whole week's allowance to buy just one! And here

Puzzy was offering to buy him TWO of the beyond-delicious delights....it was just way more than he could refuse, no matter what the consequences.

FINALLY, it was the turn of the people in line ahead of them; a tired-looking mother with three loud, demanding identical triplets, with bright red hair and upturned noses that reminded Aidan of little piglets. Very SPOILED piglets! They kept changing their minds about what they wanted; first it was regular Choco-Cheezies. Then they decided they'd rather have the deep-fried variety. And then, after their orders had been placed, they changed their minds again; this time to Choco-Cheezies with Chewy Chopped Cherries! Their mother looked as if she wanted to cry. Aidan knew exactly how she felt—he'd just glanced at Puzzy's watch and discovered that it was 10:25; only five minutes left!

Eventually the three little whiners and their tired mother got their orders and left the line. "What would you boys like?" asked the cashier. "Ummm...." said Puzzy, looking glassy-eyed at the lengthy options on the menu posted behind her. "Wow! You can add sprinkles or marshmallows now? Cool!" "Yeah," said the cashier, "and crushed cookies and peppermint flakes, too!" "Just four regulars," burst out Aidan. "C'mon, Puzzy....they're plenty sweet already!" "Heeeey," protested Puzzy, "Who's paying for this, anyway?" But he didn't cancel the order, and thirty seconds later, they were both handed their sweet, cheesy, gooey treats. Aidan took a big bite of one of his Choc-Cheezies and then thanked Puzzy for being so generous....and he really meant it, too. But he could see by Puzzy's watch that he was now down to just three minutes before his family's favorite TV show was going to end. He felt terrible about doing it, but he just HAD to get away from Puzzy, and any other prying eyes.

Shoving his Choco-Cheezies into the other pocket of his coat that didn't hold the Teleportraveling Bowl, he slapped Puzzy on the shoulder with an enthusiastic "Thanks, Dude!" and then took off toward the non-stop stream of people out in the mall's concourse. He could hear Puzzy yelling out his name behind him as he disappeared into the crowd of shoppers, and he felt really bad to be literally eating and running. He would make it up to Puzzy back at school on Monday by giving him his cafeteria desserts for a week, but for now, he HAD to find someplace private and FAST, in order to get back home in time with the Teleportraveling Bowl!

Aidan ducked into the first Men's Room he saw and ran into the nearest stall, slamming and locking the door behind him. Did he still have time to get home undiscovered? Would the bowl even work without Nonna here? There was no time to think...he brought out the bowl from his pocket and shoved two of his fingers into the purple muck inside and then into his mouth. "Yuck!" he gagged....he'd forgotten to think of a different taste for the nasty stuff, and it tasted like a combination of soap, pickles, and fireplace ashes! Or at least what he assumed that would taste like...at any rate, it was beyond gross! But there was no time to think about it. Aidan forced himself to swallow the icky blob and then somehow managed to choke out a squeaky "Eamus turpis!" Once again, the room began to spin, and Aidan squeezed his eyes shut as tight as he possibly could   while holding onto the little bowl. Either it was growing really quickly, or he was shrinking. Either way, this was...WAY...TOO...COOL!!!!

And then, suddenly, somehow, he was back again in his very own kitchen, safe and sound, and Nonna Esmeralda was quietly calling his name. Aidan opened one eye and saw that it was only just the two of them there, while his family's voices trailed in from the other room, discussing the program that had just ended. Nonna Esmeralda gave him a big smile, and then took the Teleportraveling Bowl from his hands, putting it carefully into the big yellow and pink zebra-print purse that she had brought into the kitchen while he was gone. "I will give it back to you later, caro mio...you did very well! Did you enjoy your first journey?" Aidan didn't have time to answer her before his family returned to the kitchen. "Well, you two look as if you have some big secrets!" said his father, winking. "Care to share?" Aidan stared at his grandmother, but she just gave both him and his father a big, sunny smile. "Secrets? Ah, no...no secrets. We have just been sharing stories of how much we both love to travel and of the places that we would love to see someday. I think that Aidan is going to be a great world traveler!"

Aidan's brother, Hayden, laughed. "Aidan will be lucky if he travels further than the River Front Mall--he's scared to ride his bike past the end of the block!" Aidan couldn't resist. He reached into his pocket and pulled out the unbitten Choco-Cheezie. It was still warm, and he put it into his brother's hand with a big smile. "Maybe you don't know everything." he said with a wink for his speechless brother and then another for Nonna Esmeralda, who watched, smiling. "Whaaaa...?" spluttered his brother, looking down at the Choco-Cheezie in his hand. "Where the heck did you get this???" Nonna came to his rescue; "Like your brother said, Hayden, maybe you don't know everything. Maybe none of us do. And isn't life wonderful that way?" Hayden still looked very confused, but decided to leave the room before his parents saw the forbidden Choco-Cheezie.

"Shall we get lunch going?" said his mother, and she and Auntie Maria started bustling around the kitchen. "How about you and I go take Gypsy for a walk before lunch, Aidan?" said his father, snapping a leash onto the little dog's collar. "That is a very good idea," said Nonna Esmeralda, as she tied the strings of her apron around her middle. "I think that Aidan is a boy who needs to keep on moving....a boy who really enjoys travelling!" She winked at him before turning towards the counter where a big bowl of fruit awaited peeling. Aidan smiled to himself as he, Dad and Gypsy went out the kitchen door. "Yes," he thought, "yes, indeed. I AM a boy who REALLY enjoys travelling!!!"

My English Teacher is a Secret Agent

My name is Buddy Green and I am in third grade. My best friend Willy Walters and I found a snake in the brook behind the school and put it in Miss Staples desk at lunch. It was hilarious, until Becky Mitchell told Miss Staples who she saw doing it, and we got sent to the principal's office. Becky was sore because she likes Willy, and Willy would rather hang out with me than with her.

Someone we would not try to scare is Mr. Craig, who teaches English. Mr. Craig is a Secret Agent. I know what you are thinking - but it's true. Willy and I know it for a fact.

Mrs. Jackson was our English teacher, and last fall, she had to leave school. She told the class that she had to have an operation, and that we should write her notes and tell her how school was going. She said that it would be good practice for the writing that we would be doing this year. So, when we got to English class one day, Mrs. Jackson was gone. Mr. Craig was there in her place. He is very tall and skinny. His suits are dark, and he always wears a tie. He has these shiny shoes, which just peek out from under the bottom of the pant legs, and this little shiny, black mustache- that he twirls when he is looking out the windows of the classroom.

Mr. Craig doesn't talk a lot like Mrs. Jackson did. She used to tell us about her kids, and their kids who would be her grandkids. She told us about making caramel apples for the trick-or-treaters and her husband's bad knees, "ever since he was in Uncle Sam's Army," she said. She told us about how fond she was of apple-picking season and how she was going with her husband to look at lawnmowers at Sears "n'Roebuck's."

That day, Mr. Craig waited until we all sat down. It was very quiet when Mr. Craig finally said, "Greetings." We all watched and waited, and Mr. Craig did too. He looked at us with a funny half-smile, like he was waiting for us to tell him a really funny joke.

It was only after waiting what seemed like an hour, that he began to speak.

"I am Roger Craig. I will be covering for Mrs. Jackson while she is away. I will be your English teacher." He turned and walked toward the windows. He stood looking out, and the rest of us looked too. I couldn't see what he was seeing. It just looked like the parking lot, and some clumps of trees.

He stood there looking out, and I wondered if he had forgotten about the class. If maybe he forgot that we were all looking at him. Then, without turning back, he said, "I feel that English is best taught, not by speaking it but rather by studying it. I have little to no tolerance for disruptions nor anything that prohibits this from being an environment of learning. Should we confront any, shall we say, barriers to that process, I will spare no measure to prevent it from reoccurring." With this he turned back away from the window, looking at us with the same creepy smile.

"Ordo ab chao..."

We all stared at the teacher. Nobody said a word, and I think that Willy might have been holding his breath.

"Mrs. Jackson said that you are all reading "The Diary of Anne Frank"- why don't you all take the next 20 minutes for quiet reading time before I quiz you on chapters 3 and 4 tomorrow."

No, Mr. Craig doesn't say much. That is okay with me. When he does speak to you, he looks at you, really looks at you like he knows all about you. Like he could tell that you had a frosted strawberry pop tart for breakfast and that you like the way Jenny Washerstein braided her hair with little purple beads for gym. Willy and I always hoped that he wouldn't talk to us- that he wouldn't look at us- so we kept our heads down when Mr. Craig would walk up and down the aisle during quiet reading time or when he was looking for a volunteer.

One day, I happened to peek up to see where he was and he caught me looking at him. Mr. Craig looked right at me with that smile that scares Willy. He cocked his head and touched his mustache. "Buddy... Please read the next sentence, and tell me which adjective describes the noun?"

"Uh...uh..." I tried to find the sentence that we were working on, and then I stuttered, "The old man is tired of his job... old... the man is old...Right?" Mr. Craig gave me one of his looks, and locked his eyes on me. "I don't know, Buddy. Is he?" Everyone in class laughed. I felt my face get hot, and blurted, "He's probably tired because he is too old to work!"

Mr. Craig had started to walk away from me toward the windows, probably to do some more mustache twirling, when he stopped. He turned around on his heels quickly and the class got quiet.

"Why, Buddy... it is a foolish man indeed that criticizes the endeavors of another. Things are often not as they appear. Labor omnia vincit..."

When he finally looked away and had moved on to the next sentence, I slunk way down in my seat. He picked Melissa King and she acted like that was some big thrill.

"He's weird, "I told Willy that day on our way home from school. "The way he keeps touching his mustache and talking in French... It's stupid." Willy had been my best friend since the summer before we started kindergarten. Willy was smaller than me, with glasses, but he was one of the smartest kids I knew. Sometimes kids tried to give him a hard time, but I always stuck up for him. And in return, Willy sometimes did my math.

"He acts like he knows something that we don't know...some big secret or something..." Willy was hurrying to keep up with me. "And it's Latin, not French."

Willy and I quickly forgot all about Mr. Craig, his Latin, and his secret when we got to my house. We had serious video games to play and serious grilled cheese and pickle sandwiches to eat. Seriously.

Later that week, we were doing what Mr. Craig loved most, "quiet reading time" when an announcement came over the intercom. "Buddy Green, please come to the school secretary's office please. Buddy Green, to the office... "I looked at Mr. Craig, and he looked back. Then he nodded his head at me, and I scurried. I strolled the empty hallways littered with backpacks and loose papers, down the long corridor to the office. I moved pretty slowly, because I was not in a hurry to go back to Anne Frank.

As I approached the office, I was gawking out the tall, arched windows to the entrance and parking lot. Parked off to the side was the longest, blackest car I'd ever seen. It had dark windows, and shiny chrome trim. You couldn't see the driver, but you imagined him to be impressive.

As I rounded the turn and went in the office, a large man was exiting. He brushed by me, barely giving me a glance. I caught a whiff that smelled like my Uncle Morty when he smokes his cigars after dinner. The man was dressed in a suit with a dark hat pulled over his forehead. He reminded me of the guy in this old television show, The Menacing Man. Willy and I watched the old reruns sometimes. It was in black and white and you never got to see The Menacing Man's face.

I didn't have time to think about it anymore before Ms. Hannigan, the school secretary, startled me. "Buddy! Don't dally so. You need to call your mother. She said it's important, so I called you down." She slid a phone across the countertop in my direction. My mother's voice answered on the first ring.

"Oh, Buddy- good, dear. You will need to go to Willy's after school; I have already cleared it with Clara. I have the ladies over this afternoon, and I need you to be-well, gone. Okay, dear?" This didn't bother me, as I had met the ladies, and was not too crazy about an afternoon with them either. When Mom and I hung up, I saw Ms. Hannigan looking out the windows, through the blinds, toward where I had seen the mysterious vehicle parked. She didn't look at me as she said, "Buddy, you go back to class now. Go on back to Mr. Craig's class. Don't dally..."

I skipped back to class thinking of what Willy and I might have planned for the afternoon. As I came to the end of the long hall toward my English class, I drew in a breath. Way down the hall, I saw the distinct profile of a large, imposing figure. It was the man from the office! He was leaning against the doorframe of Mr. Craig's room talking with none-other than Mr. Craig. The large man handed something to Mr. Craig and then it was gone- vanished. I moved closer, pulled by curiosity but heavy with nervousness. When I was close enough so I thought I might slip by the two men unnoticed, Mr. Craig looked me square in the face. "Why, Buddy. I do hope everything is all right at home. Go back to class. Don't dally."

I scampered by the two men silently, slipping in the doorway and hurrying to my seat. Everyone was hunkered over their papers, the only sound was of the pencils scratching against them. How did he know? How did Mr. Craig know that I got a call from home? And why did he tell me not to dally- just like Ms. Hannigan said when I was leaving...?

Mr. Craig quietly came into the room, closing the door behind him. I wondered where the mysterious package was- there were nothing in his hands and no unusual bumps or humps in his dark suit that I could tell. I pretended to be very interested in my work, hoping to blend in. After what seemed like a few minutes, I dared to slowly peek up toward where I thought Mr. Craig might be sitting, or reading, or looking out the windows, and he was looking right at me. He gave me his creepy half-smile. And then he winked.

"Willy, there is something not-right with Mr. Craig. That guy he was talking to looked shady. Like some kind of criminal." Willy and I were headed to his house to make chocolate milkshakes with the antique milkshake machine that Willy's mom always let us use. We liked to hang out at his house and bug his sister and little brother. I was an only child, so this was something I didn't get to do when we hung out at my house.

"Hey let's hide someplace and scare your sister." I said, knowing Willy would do pretty much whatever I wanted to do. "Okay. John Carlisle said that he had late practice for the band and he saw Mr. Craig there. It was like nine o'clock at night. Why would he still be at school?"

I spotted a grasshopper on the side of Willy's porch, and I carefully moved hoping to catch him and bring him in the house to meet Willy's little sister. "I'll tell you why" I said, slowly cupping my hands toward the grasshopper. "Because he is one strange bird..." With that, the grasshopper scampered away, escaping into the grass.

The next day when we got to Mr. Craig's class, he was sitting at his desk with his hands folded neatly across his middle. He was never sitting at his desk when we came in. He usually was standing at the door meeting us when we entered, or he would be standing in his mustache-twirling position by the windows.

"Greetings" he said when we all sat down. We all sat and looked at him, waiting for him to tell us to open up Anne Frank and do our "quiet reading time." He kept looking at us for what seemed like forever with that stupid half-smile on his stupid face. Then he said, "Today we are going to do something a bit different... Something more- uh, interactive." That definitely did not sound like a good idea to me. Even though I wasn't crazy about quiet reading, I was sure that I would like this interactive thing even less.

"English is not only about reading, vocabulary, and literature, but it also entails public speaking and a firm grasp of the language. That is, to speak articulately and use proper conversational English is important also." Mr. Craig looked way too happy about this. He went on, "So, I am going to request volunteers and ask them to individually stand and address the class with a succinct introduction and presentation on a hobby or past-time that you enjoy. In proper

English language and classroom appropriate manner. I will keep track of the time with this," he held up a small round watch on a chain attached somewhere under his dark gray suit. "How does that sound?"

The room was silent. It was so quiet; you could hear Billy Barton's stomach growling in the second to last row. I didn't dare to breathe, afraid that I would become Mr. Craig's first "volunteer." Mr. Craig must have heard Billy's stomach rumbling too, because he was the first one picked.

"Billy, would you please stand?" Billy looked like he had been caught doing something he shouldn't. "Would you please introduce yourself to the class and tell us about something you enjoy?" Mr. Craig was walking up and down the aisle with the fist up under his chin, like he was really concentrating on what Billy had to say.

"But everyone in class already knows who I am" Billy looked confused.

"Oh, I realize that but it is appropriate to introduce yourself before asking them to listen to the words you are about to speak." Billy stared blankly at Mr. Craig. "Let's move on, Billy- how about telling us in a couple sentences about an activity that you enjoy... Can you do that?"

What Billy liked to do was eat. He was the one kid I knew that got the hot-lunch in the cafeteria that liked it. Loved it so much that he always went back for seconds. He tried going back for thirds until the lunch lady drove him away. Right now, Billy's stomach was reminding him that it was almost time for lunch.

"Uh, er, well I like to, uh, er... I, uh, like, uh..." Billy stammered.

Mr. Craig held up his hand.

"Stop! The underlying assignment is to speak articulately and engage your peers. That is not happening... You can sit down, Billy..." Billy looked relieved and embarrassed.

Mr. Craig seemed to be getting a little cranky about how this was going. "Okay, everyone. Oral presentations are a part of life. You need to work on presenting yourself in a coherent and succinct manner... Here, like this..." Mr. Craig cleared his throat, and then turned to face the class. "Hello. I am Mr. Craig and I teach English. I enjoy world travel, and martial arts. I have black belts in Tai Kwon Do and Ju Jitsu and study under a sensei at a Dojo in Shanghai. There. That's a cohesive, congruent statement..."

"Is that true?" I didn't even realize that I had chimed in. I don't know who was more surprised, me or Mr. Craig from the look that suddenly crossed his face. It was a mix of irritation and amusement. I had seen that look before, usually from my mom.

The class was still as Mr. Craig looked at me. After a minute, he said something that gave me a very weird feeling. "It is the foolish that critique the work of others, Buddy. Labor omnia vincit..." And then he smiled.

Willy and I were walking to school the next morning talking about our teacher's strange behavior. Things just didn't add up. It was then that Willy had an idea.

"I've got it! I figured it out... Mr. Craig has got to be a spy. Speaking in Latin, the karate, that creepy guy you saw... He must be here on some kind of spy mission..." Willy looked quite pleased with himself for having solved the mystery of Mr. Craig.

I wasn't so sure. "Why would a spy pretend to be a teacher? That seems dumb." And then it hit me. "Unless he's a secret agent. That has to be it!"

It was just as I had figured this out that we got to the crosswalk by the school parking lot. Slowly pulling in past us was a shiny red Porsche. Willy and I both stopped to stare. Then I saw who was driving: it was Mr. Craig! That cinched it.

"Wow...." was all I could say. Willy looked at me knowingly.

"Maybe it's a sign. An omen. Seeing him drive by in a car like that... No teacher drives a Porsche! He has got to be a secret agent! It's like when a bird poops on your head, Buddy... it's supposed to be a sign of good luck. That was our sign of good luck. Our sign that our English teacher is a special agent..."

"Wait a minute" I said. "A bird pooped on your head?"

And then, he was gone. The following Monday morning after Willy and I saw Mr. Craig driving the secret agent car, we got to English class and Mrs. Jackson was sitting behind her desk smiling from ear to ear.

"Helllooo! Hellloooo, everyone... I missed yoooou..." She

sang at us as we came in. I stood by my desk and couldn't help but ask, "Wait. Where's Mr. Craig? I thought he was going to be here a while because of your operation..." She looked crushed. She straightened up in her chair and wasn't singing anymore.

"Well, it's lovely to see you as well, Buddy. Actually, Mr. Craig has accepted another assignment that will be taking him out of the country for a while, that's what administration told me. I came back early, because of Mr. Craig's commitment and because my doctor thought I was doing so well. I appreciate your concern." She didn't seem chipper anymore.

"Mr. Craig left word here that you all really benefit from "quiet reading time" during class, so maybe that's what we'll do. Why don't you get out "Anne Frank" and get started..."

Mr. Craig never came back to be a teacher at our school. Or maybe he did, but I just didn't recognize him. A secret agent has to be a master of disguise. I might not know him by his clothes, or his hair, or even his twirly mustache, but I am sure that I would remember that half-smile of his. It's not every kid that can say their English teacher is a secret agent. Is yours?

The Mysterious Window

Once upon a time there was an old, quaint house that stood near the woods. It was a big house where the winds blew in the autumn leaves and the moon shone on the glass windows. Around the house a yellow fence ran in a perfect square, broken only in one spot near a corner. It is here in this break in the fence that Samantha first saw things through the Mysterious Window.

Samantha was born and raised in the city with her younger brother Lewis. They lived in an apartment on the 8th floor of a high building with their parents. Samantha and Lewis knew all the streets on their block but rarely played outside their apartment. Sometimes the cars went too fast through the neighborhood.

Sometimes the smoke and the fog mixed together and it was hard to breathe outside. Sometimes it rained and the gutters overflowed. And there were times, in the night, that short explosions and other loud noises would wake up Samantha and she had to go to her mom to sleep.

Her father was a soldier working in another country. He stayed there for many months and years, coming home only for days or weeks. Samantha learned not to expect him too much on important occasions like her birthday or Christmas. When he did come, it was always a pleasant surprise. In his last stay, he had given her a red and gold ring for her birthday. It was very pretty and she wore it always.

One day in summer, in the middle of the school vacation, her mother went over to Samantha and told her they're going on a short vacation.

"We'll be going over to Uncle Samuel for two weeks."

"Why?" Samantha asked.

"Well, he's broken his leg and he might need help for a few days. Anyway, it's nice in the country this summer. We could all do a little out of town trip."

Samantha wasn't so sure. She liked being indoors and reading books or watching her favorite channel. Lewis likes being outdoors, so he probably would be happy about the trip.

On their way to their uncle's house, Samantha watched the sun follow them on the road. It had been many years since they went to their Uncle Samuel's house. She could not remember much about the old house, and wondered what their uncle looked like. She remembers that Uncle Sam had blue eyes and a warm smile, though he wore odd clothes and spoke with an accent. Samantha wondered how his leg got broken.

Samantha thought about this until the passing buildings and highway signs along the road made her tired and sleepy and she closed her eyes.

"An eagle!"

"Be a little more quiet Lewis, your sister's sleeping."

"But there's an eagle, I saw it!"

Lewis' loud voice woke up Samantha, and she was surprised to see a blur of green going by the car window. There were many tall trees beside the roads, and she could see more of them ahead. They must have left the city already and was getting closer to Uncle Samuel's house.

Uncle Samuel lived alone by the woods, and had never visited them in their house in the city. Her mom says that Uncle Samuel loved the woods and would not live away from it for any reason.

Their car turned at an intersection and after a few crossroads they saw a tall house in a neat courtyard with a perfect square, yellow fence running around it. They had arrived.

Samantha opened the door and stepped out. It was oddly quiet in here, as if the trees kept out the noise of the outside world. She helped her mom and Lewis carry their things to the front door. On the welcome mat, there was a red leaf. Samantha stared at it. There was never a leaf, red or otherwise, on their welcome mat in their apartment.

The door was opened and a slightly tall, brown man stepped out and hugged her mother. Samantha immediately looked at his broken leg. He was wearing pants and there were no bandages in sight. Perhaps they were underneath the clothes. His uncle hugged Lewis, then bent down carefully to her height and welcomed her.

"Hello, Sam. Welcome back. I'm so glad you could come."

Samantha smiled and allowed herself to be hugged. Her uncle smelled differently, as if he spent a lot of time in the sunshine and the wind. They went in and unpacked their bags. The house was big and comfortable, and she could see why Uncle Samuel stayed here a lot. It was quiet and clean and she felt free in a different way.

Lewis immediately went outside to play. She watched him from her upstairs window, where she and her mother would sleep. Outside the window the forest seemed like a sea of green, with blue mountains behind them. Samantha stared at them until it began to grow dark, then she closed the window just as the sun became red and orange.

At dinner, their mom cooked for them. She had also bought food and other stuff for Uncle Samuel. He smiled at them and asked them about their studies while eating. They played some board games that Uncle Samuel took from a big wardrobe in his bedroom. When it was time to sleep, she helped her uncle up the stairs to his room. He thanked her and asked her if she liked her room.

"It's okay," she said.

"And what can you say about the forest?" he asked.

"Uh, it's okay. The forest is so big."

"Yes, yes." His uncle swung his leg on the bed a little heavily. He said, "A long, long time ago a boy stayed in that room and he grew to love it." He smiled again. "He saw something through that window that no one else saw."

Samantha thought about the boy and what he saw through the window, but decided not to ask. She said good night and went to their room. As Samantha was tired from the journey, she fell asleep quickly and dreamed of the boy and the window.

The next day, Lewis had gone out as soon as breakfast had finished. Samantha looked for books to read inside the house, but her uncle only had old magazines and some newspapers. It's clear he stayed in here a lot. So, finding no good books to read, she decided to look outside for something to do. She went out the front door and saw that the red leaf was still there. It was a big leaf with a tapered, pointed tip. She tiptoed carefully past it and stepped into the front yard.

There were a few trees with vines of flowers around them that looked pretty. Aside from a wooden chair in the middle of the lawn, nothing else can be seen. The grass had grown up to her ankle and needed to be cut soon, she thought. A little far away she could see the thick forest surrounding them. Samantha walked over to the trees, looking at the flowers. She heard birds but did not see them.

While she was looking up at the flowers high in the branches, she caught sight of a red dragonfly hovering above. It was a rather big, strong dragonfly and both his eyes and wings were red. Samantha watched him land on a blade of grass, slowly lowering his wings close to his body. When she tiptoed close to him, he flew away. Samantha followed him for a while around the yard, and it seemed like he was playing with her. Finally he flew very high and went over to the forest. When he went away, Samantha felt tired and went inside.

It was only at dinner that she noticed her ring was missing.

She was lifting her fork to eat a piece of chicken when she saw that the ring was not on her finger.

"Oh!" she said. "What is it?" her mother asked. "My ring-the one that Daddy gave-it's gone!"

Samantha put her fork down, very upset but holding back her tears.

"Where did you lose it?" asked Uncle Samuel. "I don't know. I was looking for books earlier and then I – I went outside." "You must've dropped it outside," Uncle Samuel said. "Can I look for it?" Samantha asked her mom.

"No, it's late already and anyway it's too dark. You can look for it tomorrow."

Samantha did not feel like eating after that. That ring was her favorite and maybe her father would be angry if he knew she lost it. She began to feel cross coming here. If only she had not chased that dragonfly, perhaps she would still have the ring.

Uncle Samuel watched her closely during dinner and until it was time to go to bed. When it was time to sleep, Samantha tried not to think of the ring too much.

The next morning, Samantha ran outside right after breakfast. It was hard looking in the grass and she could not find her ring. It was just a small ring, and the yard was so big.

She looked all morning, but when lunchtime came she still did not find it.

"Have you found your ring, Sam?" Uncle Samuel asked her.

"No," she answered sadly.

He said nothing for a while, then went up to his room carefully. When he came down he smiled at her and said, "Come on, I'll help you find it."

"But your leg, Uncle?"

"I'll be fine, don't worry."

From the kitchen her mother told them to be careful. Uncle Samuel went with her outside, and he seemed to wake up in the sun and the wind. He asked her where she had gone the day before, and she showed him the places where she stopped to look at the flowers and the trees. They followed the path she took the day before, but they did not find the ring.

Samantha felt very upset and there were tears in her eyes already. It seemed they would never find her ring again.

But Uncle Samuel smiled and took something from his pocket.

"I guess we'll have to use the Mysterious Window," he said.

Samantha felt surprised when she heard that. What is a Mysterious Window?

Uncle Samuel held something in his hand and went back to the starting point of the path. Then he lifted up something to his eye, an ordinary square piece of wood with a small hole in it. He peered into it and looked at the ground again. Samantha wanted to ask him questions about how the square wood with the small hole would help them in search of her ring, but she was curious and followed her uncle while he slowly walked around the yard with the "window" to his eye.

For a time he said nothing, looking intently at the grass. Then, near the tree with flowers where she first saw the dragon fly, he seemed to see something in the ground and bent down to pick it up. It was her ring.

"Oh!" Samantha said, very surprised.

"Here's your ring, Sam," Uncle Samuel said. He gave it to her.

Samantha took the ring and held it tightly in her hand, afraid to lose it again. After a while, she put it on her finger, where it belonged. The red and gold sparkled in the sun.

"Thank you, Uncle Samuel."

"You're welcome. Shall we go inside?"

Samantha wanted to ask him a hundred questions but he was already walking towards the house. So she followed him inside, thinking about the Mysterious Window.

Later, after dinner, her uncle was sitting in the living room reading some old magazines. When her mother wasn't looking, Samantha went up to him shyly. His uncle seemed to know that she wanted to ask something and told her to sit on one of the chairs.

"Uncle?"

"Yes, Sam?"

"How did you..." Samantha took a deep breath. "How did you find my ring?"

He smiled. "Well, you saw me use the Mysterious Window, right?"

"But it's just..."

"What?"

She hesitated, then said it. "It's just a piece of wood with a hole in it."

Uncle Samuel looked at her for a while, then smiled. "Oh no, Sam. It's not just a piece of wood. It's a Mysterious Window. Only a few people see it and know how to use it." He smiled at her as if he knew a secret. "People only see what they choose to look at, and they look at only what they think is important. That's how the Mysterious Window works"

"Can I see it?"

Her uncle took it out and gave it to her. Samantha examined it in her hands. What would she see inside? Perhaps the Mysterious Window would show invisible fairies or angels that she could not see. Maybe it was like X-ray, and she would see through things. Or maybe it was like a magic microscope, magnifying small things so she could see the tiniest particles. Excitedly, she put it in front of her eye and peered in.

The hole was small and the wood blocked out the edges of her vision. But, besides that, there was nothing else. She saw the same room, the same furniture, the same Uncle Samuel. No fairies or X-ray. No microscope. She put it down disappointedly.

"Well, what did you see?" her uncle asked.

"Nothing. It was all the same. There's nothing mysterious about it." Maybe the Mysterious Window worked only with Uncle Samuel.

"That's because you're looking through it wrong." Uncle Samuel did not seem disturbed by her discovery.

"Try it again tomorrow outside and tell me what you see."

Samantha agreed, but inside she knew there was no mystery with the Mysterious Window.

Early next morning, Samantha got up before her mother and brother did and went outside. It was still a little dark, but she could not wait to see if the Mysterious Window worked outside. Uncle Samuel found her ring, didn't he? She stood in the middle of the yard and put the Mysterious Window to her eye. Then she looked down and walked around, looking at her feet and the ground.

She saw the same grass and her shoes, and was about to give up when she ran into something hard. She saw the old, yellow fence in front of her shoe and noticed the broken ends of the wood planks. Something in the broken wood caught her eye.

Without taking away the Mysterious Window from her eye, she slowly kneeled down and examined it. The wood plank was broken clean through, and the yellow paint on the surface was peeling off. But the wood underneath it was light brown, and something dark stood out against it. She moved her eye and the Mysterious Window closer and saw that it was a tuft of red and white fur.

Samantha was surprised, and with the discovery of the red and white fur she began to see other things. Different shapes and color seemed to leap out from the green grass and the things in it. She saw perfectly round dew on tips of the blades, some with little bits of twigs and leaves in them. The wood of the broken had interesting patterns and she saw spots of rough brown where the paint did not cover it. Interestingly, the ground itself seemed to show her a thousand little things that she did not see before.

At breakfast, Uncle Samuel noticed her wide eyes and knew what she was thinking.

"Well, Sam, what did you see?"

She was silent for a while. Then she told him. "I saw something by the fence," she said. Lewis and her mother were looking at her. Uncle Samuel smiled and told her to continue. "There were twigs and bits of leaves inside the dew drops, and the fence was not all painted yellow. There were some small spots where the wood showed."

"Really?"

"Yes. And there was yellow powder on some of the grass, and dust too."

"You saw dust?" Uncle Samuel asked her.

"Yes. And there was- there was red and white fur on the broken part of the fence."

Uncle Samuel looked pleased. "Hmm, the Mysterious Window seems to be working now."

"Is it?"

"Yes. Try it again on a different place and tell me what you see."

For several days Samantha used the Mysterious Window on every part of the yard. It still seemed to be an ordinary piece of wood with a hole in it, yet she was seeing new things every day that she did not see with her eyes alone. One time she saw broken blue eggshells on a spot she passed before. Another time, she saw a perfect little white down feather resting lightly on a grass tip. She told all these things to Uncle Samuel and he always said the same thing. "Go outside and use it and tell me what you see."

A few days later, Uncle Samuel took off the bandages on his broken leg. He seemed strong enough with all the rest and the meals cooked by Samantha's mom. He now used a cane to walk around. On the second to the last day of their stay with him, he went outside with Samantha.

They looked again around the yard, and Samantha couldn't believe that Mysterious Window would still show something new every day, but there was. After they had gone around, they rested under the tree where she had lost and found her ring. Then, the red dragonfly flew overhead.

"He's here again!" Samantha cried.

"Who?" Uncle Samuel asked.

"The red dragonfly." She blushed a little. "I was chasing him the day I lost my ring."

"Ah, so that's how it happened." They watched the

dragonfly zoom and glide through the air, and the red of his wings glistened brightly in the sun.

Then, amazingly, another dragonfly joined him out of nowhere.

"Look! There's another red dragonfly!" cried Samantha.

"Hmm, it seems it's that time of year again," observed Uncle Samuel.

"What do you mean?"

"Help me up and I'll show you." Samantha helped him up and together they stepped over the broken part of the fence and went out to the forest.

At the very edge of the forest, a small pool of water had formed in the ground. It was strewn with leaves and the ground around it was soft and wet. Uncle Samuel kneeled down carefully and told Samantha, "Tell me what you see."

Samantha looked into the small pool. "I see leaves in the water."

"And?"

"Some broken twigs and small branches, and some rocks."

"Is that all?"

Samantha squinted her eyes. "Yes, that's all."

"Alright. Now look through the Mysterious Window."

Samantha took the Mysterious Window out and put it in front of her eye. She leaned closer and immediately the Mysterious Window showed her a dozen things she hadn't seen before. She described them as she saw them.

"I see a small insect walking on the water," she reported.

"That's a water strider," answered Uncle Samuel.

"His legs are making ripples on the water. I see something green and white clinging to the leaves." Samantha kept her eyes on the pool. "I see small bubbles floating freely, some sticking to the leaves. I also see sunlight reflecting on the water. It looks like gold and diamonds-something brilliant."

"You still haven't seen it."

Samantha looked up. "Didn't see what?"

Try again and tell me if you see something new."

Samantha described many things to Uncle Samuel, but each time he shook his head. Finally, he took the Mysterious Window from Samantha. "I guess you're ready for the next part," Uncle Samuel said. He pressed an edge of the wooden square and another lining inside the hole in the wood popped out. The hole was now smaller than ever, like the lens of a camera when it is half closed. He handed this to Samantha and pointed to the pool of water.

Samantha held up the Mysterious Window to her eye, and her field of vision was more limited than ever. At first she had difficulty adjusting, but when she looked at the small pool, she saw amazing things.

The sunlight was underwater, and small dust and particles were floating and dancing in the rays. Small round things like eggs clung to the underside of one leaf. A fallen flower had yellow powder all over its petals – like that she saw at the fence. And near the ray of sunlight, a small red net with little red things was floating in the water.

"I see it, I see it!" Samantha exclaimed.

"Very good. Describe it to me."

"It looks like a red circular net. There are little round objects stuck to it. They're also red." She had never seen anything prettier than the little red net dancing in the water.

"Do you know what those are?" her uncle asked.

"I don't know - I've never seen them before."

"They're dragonfly eggs."

"What?" Samantha was very surprised. She haven't thought at all about how dragonflies are born. It was amazing to see the dragonflies and their family nearby. Perhaps the two red dragonflies were mates.

Uncle Samuel smiled at her. "Now you know the real secret of the Mysterious Window."

She was too busy using it to see more things in the pool and the ground around it. Uncle Samuel got up and left her to explore some more of the world through the Mysterious Window.

At dinner that evening, Samantha talked freely of what she saw through the Mysterious Window. Her mother was glad she had such a good time outside. She also reminded them to pack their bags that night as they will be leaving early the next day. This made Samantha quiet. She was sad to be leaving Uncle Samuel and this place.

Later that night, Lewis asked to borrow the Mysterious

Window. Samantha told him it would be better to use it outdoors and during the day, but he was very insistent and so she let him take it. Then she started packing her clothes and stuff into her bag.

She wondered if she could stay a little longer. She had grown to love her room and the big house and exploring around with the Mysterious Window. Leaving meant she would not be able to see the secret world through it again. Samantha decided to ask her mom if they could stay a little longer, since there's still two weeks of vacation left. She went downstairs to talk to her. Just then, Lewis burst through the door. He was teary eyed and his knees were dirty.

"Sam! Sam!" he cried.

"Why? What happened?"

"I lost it."

"What?"

"I lost...I lost the Window."

"Oh, Lew! What happened?"

"I was trying to use it outside, and when I looked up from the ground I saw bright white eyes by the broken fence. It was so scary. I ran in here and when I looked for the Mysterious Window, it's gone."

Samantha ran out in the darkness and tried to feel for it in the grass. "It can't be gone, it can't be gone!"

She felt sharp rocks prick her hands and fingers but she did not give up. "It's just here, it can't be gone!" But, just like with her ring, she did not find it. That night she went to bed with a heavy heart. She did not tell her mother or Uncle Samuel that she had lost his treasured Mysterious Window. She planned to look for it first thing in the morning, before everybody wakes up.

But the next morning, her mother had woken up earlier than her to pack their things in the car and check that Uncle Samuel had everything he needed while his leg is recovering. Samantha looked impatiently outside, wishing she could run out there and find it before Uncle Samuel knew what happened. But it was not to be so.

An hour before they're set to go, Uncle Samuel walked over to her and asked if she's alright. Looking into his warm, kind face, she burst into tears and confessed that she had lost it.

"I'm so sorry, Uncle Samuel, I'm so sorry," she sobbed.

"Don't cry. We'll look for it."

But they had gone outside with Lewis and nobody found it. "How can we find it, when it's the one we use for finding things?" Samantha asked in dismay.

Uncle Samuel looked at his niece's and nephew's downcast faces, and smiled at them. "You can use the Mysterious Window anytime, anywhere," he said.

"Really?" asked Lewis.

"But it's lost!" said Samantha.

"That's easy," said Uncle Samuel. "First hold up your thumb and your forefinger." Samantha and Lewis held up their fingers like Uncle Samuel. "Then you make a circle with

61

your fingers, and you hold it up to your eyes and look through it." Samantha and Lewis did as he said. Though it was difficult for Samantha to adjust her vision as she had been using the wooden Mysterious Window, both of them found it worked like the real Mysterious Window.

"It works! Just like the real one!" said Samantha.

"Now, if you'll make the circle smaller, just by using your forefinger, you can see the second Mysterious Window." As Samantha and Lewis curled their forefinger to make a smaller hole, they began to see new things on the ground again. Uncle Samuel watched them with a smile as they looked at the ground closely and told each other what they saw. Finally their mother called them to the car. It's time to go.

Samantha and Lewis thanked their uncle for teaching them the secret of the Mysterious Window. Samantha still felt bad about losing the real one.

"Lewis said he saw bright, white eyes and he left the Mysterious Window in the yard as he ran," she said. "I would help you look for it if we had more time."

"Hmm, my old friend is back again," Uncle Samuel said.

"Your old friend?"

"Yes. Remember what you saw in the broken fence the first time you used the Mysterious Window? It was something left behind by my friend with the bright white eyes."

"Oh...you mean..."

"Yes, he's the one who broke through that fence. I was chasing after him and in the dark I didn't see the broken part.

I tripped on it and broke my leg."

"Oh! So that's how it happened!"

"Yes."

Their mother called to them to get in the car. Samantha turned to Uncle Samuel and hugged him goodbye. "Thank you for everything, Uncle. When we have holidays I'll try to come and see you."

"I'll look forward to that. Then I can introduce you to my friends in the woods."

"I'll miss you, Uncle Sam."

"I'll miss you too, little Sam."

Samantha and Lewis waved goodbye as their car drove out of Uncle Samuel's driveway. All during the drive home Samantha kept thinking of the Mysterious Window.

The next morning, Samantha's mother found her on the table looking intently at the newspaper. She was looking through the hole in her curled finger.

"What are you doing?" asked her mother.

"Mom, did you know newspaper letters are made out of small circles?" Samantha asked. Lewis was looking for something in the flower vase. "I saw it, Sam!" he yelled.

"Saw what?" their mother asked, confused by what they are saying.

And Samantha began to tell her about the Mysterious Window.

My Summer Vacation - What a Ride!

I can't believe it is the first day of fourth grade. Mrs. McNoomis smiles. She smiles a lot. Just like my mom.

You know the first day. Blah, blah, blah....what notebooks to buy for each class, which colors of markers you need for art, and don't forget the inch ruler with the metric marks on the back.

More rules, rules, rules. Feet flat on the floor. Sit up straight. Parents must sign your homework each night. There's lunch count with the three food choices. I don't eat hot lunch. I bring a bag lunch from home. No hot lunch for me. The lunch lady scares me!

Then, the first language assignment. As usual. Write a report about...no suspense here...your summer vacation! A few kids in the back moan.

Not me. This is a cinch.

It's not like I always like to write. It's just that Mrs. McNoomis says that the idea of what to write about is the hardest part. And, this time, I happen to have an idea.

Let's see now. Name in the top right corner. Peter Wilkinson. Some people call me "Pete", but I like Peter after my Grandpa. It's hard remembering all of the cursive letters.

It's not like I write lots over the summer. How do I make that capital "W"?

Grade 4. That sounds grown-up. Grade 4. Can't forget the title. Center it on the top line. "My Summer Vacation – What a Ride!"

Skip a space and indent. Now, I am ready...

* * *

It is the first day of summer vacation. Not just any day. The day. The start of the summer of all summers. The thrill I dream about. Galaxyland Amusement Park opens today at noon. You know the new amusement park in Centerville. Everyone will be there. Even Margaret. She's my friend.

Just imagine. I hear there is pink and blue swirled cotton candy. You know that sugary kind that leaves your front teeth all blue. There's a Ferris wheel that tops the trees.

The ponies are here from a ranch somewhere out west. That sounds like fun, riding round and round and maybe getting to feed a pony. I hide a few apples from the kitchen in my room, just for this day.

And, there is the roller coaster. Never been on one before.

Dad said I need to be nine-years-old. Check that one off. I turned nine in May. Almost catching up to my sister Sarah Louise who is 13 and my older brother fifteen-year-old brother, Patrick.

Dad says I need to be 54" tall. It is the average height for a 4th grader according to some health charts. For safety reasons. Guess you have to be tall enough to touch the floor of the ride. You strap a narrow belt tightly around your waist. 54 inches. How tall actually is this?

Luckily, I am pretty good at math. I take after my Uncle Johnny. He is an accountant at some investment firm. I think if 12 inches is a foot...then that would be 4 feet because 12+12+12+12 is 4 feet.

If I add that up, it is 48 inches. So then, 54 minus 48 is 6. That's 6 inches left over. That would be 4 feet 6 inches, or 4 and a half feet. Wish I could remember some of my multiplication and division facts. This would probably be an easier way.

Where did I put that roll of quarters from Grandma? Working in her vegetable garden wasn't so bad after all. Not that I really like a whole lot of vegetables. Carrots are okay and celery with peanut butter. Lettuce on ham sandwiches is fine. But, I hate, I hate spinach and Brussels sprouts and all of those green leafy things.

My hands are hurting from the weeds. But, the work is over. I have my quarters, a whole roll of them.

Better wear those cut-offs with the large side pockets. I can stuff in the pockets a few apples for the ponies. I will save one to eat later.

"Bye, Mom!" Off I go. Can't my bike go any faster? That's what I get for not reminding dad to oil the chain. There's the shortcut through Memorial Park, and down that dirt road. The road by the bridge, near my friend Margaret's house.

Whew, the line is still pretty short. Better lock my bike to the metal fence. It's close to the ticket booth. Tickets 25 cents. Pony rides $1.00. The lady with the black curls points to a sign: "Galaxyland Amusement Park invites you on an adventure to Name the Roller Coaster! Put your ideas in the box below. One entry allowed per person each day. Winner to be announced at end of summer. Special surprise waits."

I think of "Eagle-Eyed Roller Ride" and scribble down my name, too. I bet when you are on the highest track, you can see all of Centerville...my house and Margaret's, too.

Off to the roller coaster. I sprint. The line isn't very long yet. It is only 12:05 p.m. The park is open, but 5 minutes. Two-four-six-eight.....16, 18, 20...there. 20 steps to the very top.

"Next", shouts the skinny man with the leather cowboy hat. Red hair bulges from the brim. "Mr. Elliott" the nametag read. "How old are you, kid?"

I tell him I am nine. He tells me to stand under the tape. I cross my fingers and wait. "48, 49, 50, 51, 51, 52". Mr. Elliott stops at 52. "Sonny, not tall enough". I try to stand taller and push my shoulder blades back against the wooden frame of the waiting platform. If only I liked grandma's spinach. I might be a little taller. It is too late.

"Next", shouts the skinny man. It is hard to believe. No roller coaster.

A whole roll of quarters but I don't want anything else. No cotton candy – no way. I hear the kids on the Ferris wheel but I am not joining. I toss the apples down near the pony rink and bike home.

I bike slowly this time. Over the bridge, past Margaret's house. I don't care about the shortcut. I go the long way home around Memorial Park. Mom asks why I am home so early. I go to my room.

What a disappointment. Two stinking' inches! Like who really cares? Do you know how much that is? If someone gave you two inches of licorice from a licorice rope, you would think it was a joke. Just a joke!

A few days later I was watching my sister, Sarah Louise. She was getting ready for a date. A date! No way. Not for me.

I mean Margaret is my friend and all. And we do stuff together like build tree forts in the backyard. We walk our dogs at the dog park on Saturdays. We even join the same softball team. But, a date? Not for me.

I see Sarah Louise stand in front of the bathroom mirror. You know the long mirror with the golden frame. Sarah globs some stuff on her hair. She hates frizz. I hear her complain.

Hey, I have a super idea. It just might work. The bottle of de-frizz stuff says that it is guaranteed to work. You rub it in your hair. It will flatten. It will shape. You can create. I work quickly.

I pour out a large handful and pull every strand of hair on my head. I pull as hard as I can without hurting too much. I stretch my hair upward to the ceiling. Off I go to the amusement park.

I buy one ticket for 25 cents. "Crazy Blazy" I print this time. I dash up the steps.

"Next", shouts the man. It's Mr. Elliott. "How old are you, kid?"

Guess he doesn't remember me. That's a good thing 'cause he might send me away. I stand under the measuring tape.

"48, 49, 50, 51, 51 inches. Let's push the ruler down tight. Hey, kid, that's some hairdo you have. Guess you aren't as tall as I thought."

I cannot believe it. Squishing my hair like that. Using that thick, smelly gel. Why do girls like that gunk? Who knows? And then Elliott shoves 2 inches down. Hope he got a handful of that gunk on him. I know that is not nice to say. I am sorry. What will I do now?

A few weeks later, no maybe it is a more than a few weeks later. I have an idea. This one is greater than the last one. This one is sure to work. I raid mom's closet while she is shopping.

I open box after box. The fourteenth box is perfect! Navy blue pumps the box says in bold letters. 3 inch heels. Dress or casual. This works. I slip each shoe on and stuff old sports socks down near the toes. I squish the socks toward the pointy toes.

Time to go. It is a little hard riding my bike with the

high-heeled shoes. I hope no one notices.

The over-sized jeans help. At least from the front. You can't really see the heels. I suppose if you look really carefully from the back. You might see a heel.

I buy one ticket. "Glitter and Flitter" I write and add my name. After all, the roller coaster is shiny new. Bet, it moves really fast like something that flitters. I like it. "Glitter and Flitter". It has a fun rhyme to it

I slowly climb the stairs. It is hard to walk in heels, especially for the first time. I giggle.

Just when Mr. Elliott says, "Next". I do the unthinkable.

I trip.

A heel falls off my right shoe and drops down to the ground. I hear Mr. Elliott's voice, "Next".

I ride home. Mom is not there. She is still at the store. I find the super glue in the cupboard above the microwave. The glue is a little dry but I use it anyways. I squeeze enough to stick to the heel back. I find a hair blower and dry the glue.

The shoe looks new. I put away the pumps in box number 14. Sadly, I shut the closet door.

At the end of the month, I join a book club at the library. I see a science magazine for kids. On the cover is a kid about my age. He is really, really tall. I check out the magazine.

On page 7, it talks about "How to Make Stilts in Three Easy Steps". I wonder if I can do this.

I turn to page 7 so quickly that I almost rip the page. There is a list of materials needed. I skim down the list.

Wood. Tape measure. Saw. Nails. Hammer.

Dad works with me on my Boy Scout Badges. I make birdhouses and benches for sitting near a fire. Margaret and I build tree forts with old wood.

Glancing around the garage there are some long pieces of wood that possibly would work. The tape measure, a handsaw, and a pail of nails rest on the work bench.

I find a hammer under the box of nails. First, I measure the wood. A mark goes for 12 feet and then a second mark for 6 feet.

Carefully the saw makes a cut. The wood falls into equal sections. Next, two identical rectangular shapes are cut. About 6 inches by 3 inches. These attach to the longer wooden strips and are placed perpendicular to the 6 foot strips, just up a few inches from the base. I know it sounds a little complicated. I had to read it a few times.

The directions in the magazine say this is the important part. If you attach the footholds up 2 inches from one end, you will be at least 2 inches taller. You can also add the height of the footholds. I decide not to take any chances. I place the footholds 4 inches from the bottom. This will ensure extra height.

Attaching these pieces is pretty easy. Several nails do it. Now, it's practice time. Holding on to the handles, I manage to lift myself up and rest my feet on the footholds. I lift one foot up, place it down. Repeating this with the other leg takes some balance. About a half an hour later, you would never know that this is my first time.

The plan is to wear baggy, long pants. You know the kind teenagers wear these days. A baggy shirt will help cover up the arm handles. Raiding dad's closet is key to this cover up operation. Not that he is a teenager. That's funny. Thinking of my dad as a teenager. But, he is sure to have the clothes I need.

Now, it is impossible to bike with the stilts. Carrying them across my shoulder seems to work out. One hand is still available to hold the handlebars and steer.

This time my bike parks behind a tree, near the amusement park. This will have to do.

Getting dressed behind a tree is not so bad after all. If running were possible, that's what I would do. I can't wait! But, everyone knows you can't run in stilts.

First, the ticket and then hurriedly "C-R-A-Z-Y B-L-A-Z-Y". That name has been going through my head all day. Folding the piece of paper my hand I can't stop shaking. It is hard to slide the slip of paper into the box. This is exciting, big time!

Climbing carefully up each step becomes my mantra. Each step brings me a little closer to the top. Finally, the top. Mr. Elliott smiles to say, "Next". He has to place the tape on my head to measure.

Feeling confident now, but just then, my pants begin to slip, slip, and slip down towards my knees. Oh, no, what was I thinking? There's no belt. If forgot dad's belt. How could I?

Oh, that's okay. The stilts are still help tight under my arm pits. My hands are free. Grabbing my pants with one arm, before they slip even further, there is laughter around me. Some little kid behind me whispers, "Are those Sponge Bob underwear?"

There is continuous laughter. My cheeks are getting red, and more red and even more and more red.

Don't turn around, I tell myself. Next thing you know Mr. Elliott points to the next kid and shouts, "Next!"

It is now August. I think about the amusement park all the time. I dream about the roller coaster every night. I imagine every up and down, every round and round. The turns wake me up at night and there's giggling in my sleep when it's upside down.

And, then, that's when I get it. I cannot believe it. I really get it this time.

Upside Down. That's the name of Patrick's band. He's my older brother. Jamming in the basement with his friends keeps my mom and dad up at night. It's really loud music. You should have seen Margaret's face when she found out my brother is a drummer in his very own rock band.

She smiles. She thinks that it's way cool to have a friend with a brother in a rock band. We exchange smiles.

It's midafternoon and the basement is empty. Patrick is working at the neighboring sub shop. Can you say that 10 times quickly...sub shop, sub shop, sub shop?

I check out his collection of band hats. I grab lots of

them. Each says "Upside Down" on the rim.

Piling them on top of each other, this has got to add some inches. Patrick will never miss any of these hats. He has one of every color. My favorite is the bright orange one with the dark blue letters.

Now, biking to the park is a breeze. Excitement mounts. This is it. This is it. This is it. One ticket. Hmmm, what guess should be entered? "Red Rascal" is carefully written. Why, "Red Rascal", you ask?

Well, "Red" is for Mr. Elliott's hair. You know the hair he hides under that enormous cowboy hat.

"Rascal", well, I hate to admit. Rascal, because of me. I smile. You know, all those mischievous things I thought of as ways to ride the roller coaster this summer.

One ticket is bought. Flying up the steps, both hands hold down the pile of hats. Nothing will stop me now. This is the motto of the mailman...neither rain nor hail nor...you get the picture.

On the platform, Mr. Elliott asks, "You, old enough, kid?"

I nod. Well, it's actually not really a lie. I am tall enough. Tall enough with the hats.

Mr. Elliott points to the lettering on my hats. He thinks "hat" but I know better.

"That's the name of my brother's rock band. The band is called Upside Down."

"Yep, that name sounds pretty catchy. Heard it before. Aren't they playing here tomorrow for the Labor Day Bash?

Thought boss mentioned something like that."

Patrick always lucks out. His band is playing for the bash tomorrow, the last day the park is open for the season. The end of summer.

"Have you heard about the contest?"

You mean the one to name the roller coaster?

"Yup, that's the one."

I nod.

"Well, let's see what we have here. 50, 51, 52, 53, 54, looks like 55 inches. Feel free to enter, kid."

Mr. Elliott continues to chat. "I hear the wind is supposed to pick up. Do you see those dark clouds over there?" He points to the clouds.

Politely, I look to my left. I nod.

"Haven't you been watching the weather, kid?"

My shoulders shrug.

Just then, and if on cue, lightning whizzes in sharp jagged swords to light up the sky. You would think it is the Fourth of July. I love the Fourth of July.

Immediately, the announcement comes: "The Park is closing. Attention, all patrons. The park is officially closing because of inclimate weather. We will re-open tomorrow at noon for the Labor Day Bash. That is to say, if the weather cooperates."

It starts to drizzle. It begins to rain. It is soon pouring. I don't care one bit. I walk home holding the plastic handlebars of my bike with one hand.

Lucky for me and Patrick's hats. At least they keep some of the rain away. Oh, who cares anyway?

My mom and dad are watching the news. The weather man predicts a sunny day tomorrow with warm temperatures. That figures.

The local newsman adds, "Tomorrow, all across the land, a special holiday is celebrated. Labor Day. There are parades, and picnics, fireworks, and in our very own Centerville... the Labor Bash. Come to the Galaxyland Amusement Park! Doors open at noon. It is the final day of the season."

My entire family drags me to the park. After all, Patrick is booked to play.

Dad has a tough time finding a parking spot. Crowds of people wait in line to get in. Listen. Patrick's band plays.

Everyone impatiently waits to rush in for one last day. Everyone that is, but me. Don't want to be here. Nope. Don't want to be here, at all. Nope. Don't want to be here, at all, ever. Nope. I've had enough of this place.

Patrick's band stops playing. Here comes the big announcement. "And the winning entry.... to this summer's Name the Roller Coaster contest is...drum roll, please."

Patrick offers a drum roll. My dad and mom cheer. Sarah Louise even smiles. She usually is embarrassed when my parents do that. I am surprised.

"And the winning entry is 'RED RASCAL', submitted by Peter Wilkinson. Way to go, Peter!"

The crowd is cheering. This is unbelievable. Simply

unbelievable!

"The winner gets a free day today at the park. All the rides he wants. All the food he can eat. All the fun for his entire family!"

Today is the day. Yeah, it's Labor Day and all, but you know what I mean. Today, this is my day!

The photographer snaps a picture of mom and dad, and me. Mr. Elliott sandwiched me between them. He said if the lucky winner wants to ride the Red Rascal, then that's fine with him. Fine for his boss. Fine for everyone.

Dad said it is safe. There is a seatbelt and no way for me to budge out of that seat. No way. No way at all.

Anyways, the photographer is snapping pictures for the local paper. That's me in the middle. Do you see that grin?

And, this concludes my report.

I look up.

The class cheers. Mrs. McNoomis smiles.

And, I remember my summer vacation, what a ride!

Frazzle Berries

Mopsy Monkey loved her mommy. She and Mommy were best friends. They liked to play games together, and swing from the branches of their treetop home, and eat banana and frazzle berry salads.

Every day Mopsy Monkey woke up the same way. The sun would rise up and tickle her eyelids and Mopsy would laugh and jump out of her bed of leaves and clap her hands at the sun.

"Stop tickling me, sun!" Mopsy would laugh.

The sun would warm her fur and Mopsy would do backflips from branch to branch until she got down to the ground.

Every day her mommy would poke her head down and smile at Mopsy, hanging upside down from the lowest branch of the tree. "Good morning, Mopsy. I love you."

"I love you too, Mommy."

This morning Mopsy's mommy gave her a hug. Then she asked. "Should we have banana and frazzle berry salad for lunch?"

Mopsy was so excited. "Oh yes, oh yes, oh yes!" She did such a big flip that she went completely head over tail and got herself stuck up in the branches of the tree. "Oops," she said.

Mommy laughed at Mopsy and helped her down. "Go and have you breakfast, my dear. I'll start the salad for our lunch."

Mopsy was having a big bowl of fruity-rooty cereal when she heard her mother cry out. "Oh, no!"

She climbed up the tree until she got to their kitchen. There was her mommy, looking very upset.

"Oh, no, Mopsy. We're all out of frazzle berries!"

Mopsy saw the empty berry bowl. She was very sad. No frazzle berries meant no frazzle berry salad.

Then Mopsy got an idea. "Mommy," she said. "I can go and get the frazzle berries for us!"

"Are you sure?" her mommy asked. "It's a very long way."

Mopsy was very sure. She was a big monkey now and she knew that she could bring her mommy back the frazzle berries, all by herself.

Her mommy gave her a big hug. She told Mopsy to be careful. "Now you be sure to go straight to the frazzle berry trees and then come straight back home. Do you remember where the frazzle berries grow?"

"I sure do!" Mopsy answered. "They grow in the pine trees past the river. I'll be careful, Mommy, I promise!"

Mopsy was so happy to be starting out on her first big girl adventure. She made sure to bring her biggest and best berry bag with her, and then off she went. She had gone to pick frazzle berries lots of times with her mommy. She knew the way. She even knew where the biggest and sweetest berries grew. This was going to be easy and fun!

She ran down the path through the jungle. She wanted to be quick. But when she got to where Mason Monkey's house was in the big tree by the pond, Mason came out and jumped up in front of her, dancing a crazy dance.

"Wait, wait!" Mason said to her. "You can't pass by my house unless you give me a gift!"

Mopsy Monkey and Mason Monkey were good friends. He was a red little monkey, and Mopsy was a brown little monkey, but they loved to play together. Mopsy didn't have time to play today, though.

She tried to get by him by jumping and running and flipping but nothing worked. He just kept dancing around her in circles. "Mason," she said, "I have to go!"

Mason still wanted to play. "Gift first, gift first!"

Mopsy thought. What did she have that she could give him? She thought and thought, and then she had an idea. "Mason, do you like frazzle berries?"

"Oh boy, do I!" Mason did a little frazzle berry dance.

"Then I'll go and get you some. But first you have to let me go by or I can't get them for you!"

So Mason danced away up his tree, licking his lips at the thought of frazzle berries, and let Mopsy go on her way.

Mopsy kept going until she got to the river. The river was wide. How would she get across?

"What are you doing here, Miss Mopsy Monkey?" said a smiling crocodile in the water.

Mopsy squeaked like a second little rabbit. She knew crocodiles could be mean when they wanted to. She tried to keep away from crocodiles as much as she could. This one was right in front of her though. She couldn't be rude.

The crocodile smiled very nicely. "Don't be afraid Mopsy Monkey. Are you lost?"

"No. I'm not lost. I need to get across the river so I can get to the frazzle berries for my mommy."

"Oh! I love frazzle berries," the crocodiles said. "But I can't get to them because they grow so high up in the trees and I crawl on the ground."

The crocodile licked his lips. Mopsy Monkey had an idea. "Mister crocodile," she said, "would you like me to get you some frazzle berries?"

The crocodile's eyes got really big. "Oh, yes. Would I ever!"

"Well, if I get you some frazzle berries, would you take me over the river and back again?"

"Oh, I sure would. I love, love, love, love frazzle berries!"

Mopsy Monkey was a little afraid as she climbed on the back of the crocodile. She had never done this before. She held on tight and closed her eyes.

"Are you ready?" the crocodile asked. "I won't go until you're ready."

"I'm ready," Mopsy said.

Then the crocodile was off, swimming through the water, fast and smooth. The wind ruffled through Mopsy's fur. She opened her eyes and saw the world going by very fast. This was fun! This was exciting! "Whee!" she said, throwing her arms into the air.

They got to the other side of the river and Mopsy jumped off the crocodile's back to the dry land again. "Thank you, Mister Crocodile!"

"You won't forget my frazzle berries, will you Mopsy Monkey?" the crocodile asked hopefully.

"I won't!" she promised, racing off through the woods.

Not far away grew the tall frazzle berry trees. Frazzle berries were round and red and bigger than grapes but smaller than apples. They were delicious and tasted like chocolate covered strawberries. Mopsy loved them so much!

She used her best climbing skills to get to the branches all the way at the top of the trees where the berries grew. She picked only the best ones until her berry bag was full. She ate one herself as she picked the rest.

"Mmm," she said. So good!

Then she flipped down to the ground and ran back to the river. Her bag was full of berries. Mommy would be so proud!

When she got back to the river, the crocodile was waiting for her. He smiled at Mopsy. "You came back! I'm so hungry for frazzle berries!"

Mopsy wanted to keep the berries all or herself, but she had promised to give some to the crocodile for helping her get across the river. So she took out some and gave them to the crocodile.

He ate one right away, and then another, but the rest of them he gave away to his crocodile friends. They loved frazzle berries too.

The crocodile gave Mopsy Monkey a ride back across the river, licking his lips the whole way. "Mmm, frazzle berries," the crocodile said happily.

When they got all the way back across the river she jumped off the crocodile. "Thank you, Mister Crocodile!" Then she ran down the path back towards home. The frazzle berries smelled great in the berry bag she was carrying. It wasn't as full as it had been, but there were still plenty of berries for Mommy to make their salad for lunch. Mommy would be so proud of her!

Mopsy got all the way back to Mason Monkey's house. He was waiting for her. As soon as he saw her and the berry bag she was carrying he started doing another dance. "Frazzle berries, frazzle berries!"

Mopsy knew there were less berries in the bag than when she first picked them. She wanted to keep all of the ones she had left for herself. So she took out some, and gave them to Mason. He juggled them in the air while he danced.

"Thank you Mopsy, thank you!" he said. Then he took the berries up the tree. "Now my mommy and I can have frazzle berry pie for dinner tonight!"

Mopsy ran the rest of the way home. The frazzle berries smelled great in the berry bag. There were so few berries left in it now. She had wanted to keep them all for herself but

Mason Monkey and Mister Crocodile were so happy that she shared her frazzle berries with her. She had promised Mommy to bring them home to her, though. Would her mommy still be proud of her?

Mopsy Monkey climbed her way back up into her treetop home and found her mommy in their kitchen cutting up the bananas for the salad. "Hello, my dear," Mommy said. "Did you have fun getting the frazzle berries?"

"I sure did!" Mopsy told her all about Mason dancing around her, and about riding on the back of the crocodile. Then she told about how she had shared the frazzle berries. When she opened her berry bag up, there were only five frazzle berries left.

Mopsy was sad. There were only a few of the berries left that she had picked for her and mommy. But Mommy smiled and gave her a big hug. "I'm very proud of you," Mommy said. "You were a big girl today. Not because you went all the way to the frazzle berry trees and back, but because you shared your frazzle berries with those who didn't have any."

Mopsy Monkey was very happy. She hugged her mommy as hard as she could. "I love you, Mommy."

"I love you too, Mopsy. Now. Let's put these frazzle berries into the salad. I bet it will be the best tasting frazzle berry and banana salad ever."

And you know what? It really was.

Epilogue

So there you have it. These are the stories that I hear every day while walking to the bus stop.

But they don't stop there.

Me and my friends have BIG imaginations! I have a lot more to tell you, story wise, but you're gonna have to wait until I put these all down on paper again.

The school year only started about a month ago, and we have a LOT more walks to the bus stop ahead of us, with a lot more crazy, wacky stories that I'm sure will be told!

So be sure to stick around and wait for what's around the next corner. I know you'll like it! But now, I gotta go. Homework first, then I can play video games.

See ya!

You Might Also Enjoy

Angela Giroux is hard at work on more funny, whimsical, and sometimes inspirational stories that are perfect for kids of all ages. Let your imagination soar as you read her funny and imaginative tales! Be sure to check out her other books:

Funny Things I Heard at the Bus Stop Series:
Volume 1: http://www.amazon.com/dp/B0073XIR1Q
Volume 2: http://www.amazon.com/dp/B0076OKPI0
Volume 3: http://www.amazon.com/dp/B008KQA2YA
Globlins   in   the   Garden:
http://www.amazon.com/dp/B0077SAR74
The   Complete   Collection:
http://www.amazon.com/dp/B007FT5086

Please check out her website for information on other books that she has published and some that are in the works!
http://AngelaGiroux.com

Made in the USA
Lexington, KY
02 August 2014